The Little, Little House

About the story

This is a Jewish folktale from Eastern Europe. In most versions it is the village rabbi
who puts things right, or sometimes a wise neighbour. I have based my heroine, Aunty Bella,
on my mother's great-aunt. She came from the Ukraine where she was the wise woman of the village.
As in the story, everyone took their troubles to her and she always had an answer.

The Little, Little House copyright © Frances Lincoln Limited 2005
Text, illustrations and design copyright © Jessica Souhami and Paul McAlinden 2005

First published in Great Britain in 2005 by
Frances Lincoln Children's Books, 4 Torriano Mews,
Torriano Avenue, London NW5 2RZ
www.franceslincoln.com

Distributed in the USA by Publishers Group West

British Library Cataloguing in Publication Data available on request

ISBN 10: 1-84507-108-5
ISBN 13: 978-1-84507-108-0

Set in Gill Sans and Sabon

Printed in China

9 8 7 6 5 4 3 2

The Little, Little House

Jessica Souhami

F

FRANCES LINCOLN
CHILDREN'S BOOKS

Long ago, before you were even born,
there was a poor man called Joseph
who lived in a little, little house with his wife
and three children.

There was a yard in the front
with six yellow chickens
and a red rooster pecking the dirt.

And there was a field at the back
with a pretty brown cow
and a little grey goat chewing the grass.

And Joseph knew they could never be happy
in such a little, little house.

"How can we be happy?" Joseph sighed.
"We're so jammed and crammed, so squashed and squeezed.
There's no money for a bigger house. So what can I do?"

Suddenly he thought, "I know! I'll ask Aunty Bella."

Aunty Bella was clever and kind.
She listened to everyone's problems
and always gave good advice.

So the next day Joseph went to see Aunty Bella.

"Aunty Bella," he said, "we can never be happy in such a little, little house. What can I do?"

Aunty Bella just smiled.

"Go home, Joseph," she said,

"and take the six yellow chickens
into your house.

See what a difference
that will make!"

And Joseph did as Aunty Bella said.

But THIS is what happened ...

So the next day Joseph went back to see Aunty Bella.

"Aunty Bella," he said, "things are worse!

Our house is so full, it's creaking!

And the chickens are SO CHEEKY!

What can I do?"

Aunty Bella just smiled.

"Go home, Joseph," she said,

"and take the red rooster
into the house.

See what a difference
that will make!"

And Joseph did as Aunty Bella said.

But THIS is what happened ...

So the next day Joseph went back to see Aunty Bella.

"Aunty Bella," he said, "things are dreadful!

Our house is so full, it's shaking!

The chickens are so cheeky.

And the rooster's SO NOISY!

What can I do?"

Aunty Bella just smiled.

"Go home, Joseph," she said,

"and take the pretty brown
cow into the house.

See what a difference
that will make!"

And Joseph did as Aunty Bella said.

But THIS is what happened ...

So the next day Joseph went back to see Aunty Bella.

"Aunty Bella," he said, "things are terrible!

Our house is so full, it's quaking!

The chickens are so cheeky.

The rooster's so noisy.

And the cow's SO CLUMSY!

What can I do?"

Aunty Bella just smiled.

"Go home, Joseph," she said,

"and take the little grey goat into the house.

See what a difference that will make!"

And Joseph did as Aunty Bella said.

But THIS is what happened ...

So the next day Joseph went back to see Aunty Bella.

"Aunty Bella," he said, "things are impossible!
Our house is so full, it's bursting!
The chickens are so cheeky.
The rooster's so noisy.
The cow's so clumsy.
And the goat's SO SMELLY!
What can I do?"

Aunty Bella laughed out loud.

"Go home, Joseph," she said,

"and turn all the animals
out of the house.

See what a difference
that will make!"

And Joseph did as Aunty Bella said.

And THIS is what happened ...

"How peaceful it is," sighed Joseph.
"How quiet and clean.
Our house is not so little, little after all."
He smiled, "How happy we are."

And the next day ...

... Joseph went to thank clever Aunty Bella.